MEDITATED MURDER
A Dharma Mystery

By
Sachi Deleg

Copyright © 2012 Sachi Deleg

All rights reserved.

ISBN - 13: 978-1479285921
ISBN-10: 1479285927

DEDICATION

This book is dedicated to the wonderful meditation teachers I have studied with in the Tibetan Buddhist tradition, with appreciation for their wisdom, generosity, and compassion.

CONTENTS

Chapter 1	Renunciation	1
Chapter 2	Magic	11
Chapter 3	Hooked	19
Chapter 4	Feast	25
Chapter 5	Impermanence	37
Chapter 6	Desire	42
Chapter 7	Appearance	50
Chapter 8	Purification	57
Chapter 9	Illusion	61
Chapter 10	Inquiry	72
Chapter 11	Attachment	79
Chapter 12	Clarity	87
Chapter 13	Renewal	96

AUTHOR'S NOTE

This book is a work of fiction, and any similarities the characters may have to real people is purely coincidental.

CHAPTER 1

RENUNCIATION

"Nora, the monastic head shaving ceremony is coming up later today and it is creating a lot of inner conflict for me," I grumble, feeling out of sorts because I've been put in such a quandary. Before coming here from my home in Virginia I had asked my hairdresser to cut my hair quite short. However, now I am told it is *still* too long.

"I have no particular interest in being a nun, and the idea of someone shaving my head completely bald is a very disturbing prospect." For me, rather than representing a freely given offering, or a gesture of renunciation, as it is meant to be, it feels like an unwelcome and intrusive demand. "I love the monastery and I have great respect for the monastic community, but I am a "lay" person who just wants a supportive place to do a very long retreat."

"Well," replies Nora, "I don't think they want to force you, and some of the nuns do have a bit of hair, so why don't you just cut it shorter?"

I agree to a compromise, and start hacking my own hair to about half an inch long. Having the strands stand on end, splayed in all directions will have to be renunciation enough. I have appreciated being able to talk to Nora, and have felt drawn to her company since arriving here. She is a gentle person and seems steady and dependable. Cutting off her thick, dark hair doesn't appear to bother her a bit.

It is our third day of preparing for a year long meditation retreat on an isolated part of Nova Scotia's coast. It is to be done in the traditional Tibetan Buddhist style. The participants in this endeavor are myself - Rachel, three other women - Nora, Tracy, and Jema, and four men - Tom, Hector, Tharpa, and Guenther. Six of us are from various parts of the United States, Guenther is from Switzerland and Hector from Spain. We each have our own tiny room in a building designed for such an endeavor - eight single rooms, four men on one side of the building, four women on the other, one large bathroom on each side, a kitchen in the middle with a meditation hall on the second floor. A tall wooden fence surrounds two sides, the third is bounded by a forest, and a steep cliff descending to a vast bay is on the fourth side.

In our building, the retreatants with rooms facing the bay have a marvelous view of a large expanse of sparkling water, the sun dancing on the waves, seals cavorting, whales spewing plumes of spray, and fishing boats sailing by. My room, on the opposite side of the building, shares a wall with the bathroom and faces a tree covered hill rising about twenty feet from my window, thus blocking any view other than an occasional mouse emerging from the rocks. *Always meditate on that which provokes resentment.*

As I am putting the finishing touches on my shrine I look up to see our retreat master, Lama Tenzin, standing in the doorway to my room. He is a short Tibetan man with a wide face, an easy smile, and warm, dark eyes. He is wearing monastic robes, and holding a mala in his hand. "It looks like you are settling in well," he says. "That is a beautiful thangka you have over your shrine. Where did it come from?"

He is referring to a painting of a dakini, or "sky dancer" - a female representation of compassion and wisdom, that is framed by brocade cloth.

"It was a gift from a friend who brought it back from her trip to Nepal," I reply.

"I had to leave everything behind when I left India," Lama Tenzin says, "so I'm always grateful to see Tibetan art again." He turns to leave, taking a last wistful look at the painting before heading down the hall.

Lama Tenzin is an interesting person. He was raised by Tibetan refugee parents in India and has told us about playing by the side of the road while his parents worked breaking rocks all day to build the Indian highways. His parents took him to a monastery for schooling when he was six, where he learned a modest amount of English along with the Buddhist teachings.

As a young man he left this monastery and immigrated to Canada, working his way around the country by being a dishwasher and doing odd jobs. Eventually he noticed Naropa Monastery and Retreat Center in Nova Scotia by looking on the internet, and just showed up one day, not telling anyone he was a highly trained lama. After a year or so it became obvious that he was pretty special and he admitted to his status as an accomplished teacher. So, he was put in charge of our retreat since he was very familiar with the meditations, rituals and ceremonies we would be doing. He is currently housed in a small cabin outside of the fence that borders our building.

The monastery that is sponsoring this retreat is a 5 minute walk down the road from our building, and is home to about 40 monks and nuns. It is named after a famous teacher and scholar, Naropa, who was known not only for his scholarly understanding of Buddhist philosophy, but also for his direct, experiential realization of the meaning of the teachings. The monastery will supply part-time cooks as well as food and daily necessities.

Another representative from the monastery shows up at my room holding a bundle of burgundy cloth in her hands. "Hi, I'm Ani Sopa," she says, "I've volunteered to help you all try out the monastic robes."
I shove the various shrine offering bowls I've been working with over to the side of the room to allow enough space for both of us to stand in my tiny room. She hands me a bright golden shirt to put on as she begins unraveling a long piece of maroon wool. As I stand with my arms outstretched she expertly wraps the cloth around my waist in intricate folds to form a long skirt. There is something very touching about the

extensive history of these robes and the many dedicated meditation practitioners who wore them through the past centuries.

"What made you decide to become a nun?" I ask. "Well," she replies "I watched all of the people around me, especially women, get so absorbed in their work and family life that they had no time left for spiritual practice. I really appreciate being able to devote my life one hundred percent to following the path of the Buddha. I remember as a child feeling drawn to stories of saints and mystics. Here at the monastery, even doing everyday chores feels like part of my path of practice, and I get a lot of time to meditate and do personal retreats."

Ani Sopa finishes dressing me and then moves on to the next room. As much as I appreciate the monastic ideal, I feel constricted and awkward in these robes, and tomorrow plan to change to our alternative choice - tan pants and a burgundy shirt. As I look down the hall to see how the others are doing I notice that Nora and Jema seem very at home in their robes, and Tharpa, our one actual monk, will presumably continue to wear them. Although those of us participating in our retreat do not have to be monastics to enter, we do take the precepts - vowing not to kill, steal, lie, or become intoxicated by alcohol or drugs, and promising to be celibate. It all sounds so peaceful, so serene, however it turned out to be anything but.

I have worked very hard to be able to participate in this retreat. Besides taking on extra jobs, I've done without many entertainments, new clothes purchases and vacations in order to save money for this rare and precious opportunity. It was very daunting, not to mention professional suicide, to leave my psychotherapy practice for a year, and no one in my family is happy about being unable to see or talk to me for so long. (We are allowed to write one letter a week and receive mail, but no phone calls, other than emergencies, are permitted). Complete focus on this one thing has been my operating mode for months, and despite the difficulties I am very grateful to have made it.

Having spent months in retreat before, I know it has little relationship to the relaxing and peaceful time those who have never done an intensive meditation program imagine. It is hard work, and often frightening in its lucidity. However, it will be an opportunity to step out of the realm of worldly desires in order to see my own mind clearly, without distraction, and bring clarity to

the ways I author my own distress and,
potentially, my own contentment.

Tomorrow will be the ceremony for symbolically
locking the gate - meaning that thereafter we are
to stay in the boundaries of our building and the
small plot of land it sits on for the next year.
Presumably the helpers coming from the
monastery will take care of our daily needs.

I've been taking advantage of our last moments
of freedom to explore the surrounding property
and neighboring monastery. It is a sprawling
building with a brightly painted door and
colorful prayer flags in the front and the back.
Monks and nuns are busily going about their day,
taking care of the ordinary maintenance of
keeping everyone fed and housed. Everyone
gathers for group meditation in the morning and
evening, but most residents also have some sort
of work responsibilities.

I discovered a box of free clothing in the
monastery basement and found a nice burgundy
sweater that I thought Guenther might like.
Though he is from Switzerland, he seems
woefully unprepared for the freezing winds that
will be whipping off of the bay. He is a young

man with a wiry build and I can imagine the winter gales going right through him.

"Ungh." That was the response I got when I offered Guenther the sweater. Not exactly the gratitude I was hoping for. 'Oh well,' I thought, 'give without expectation,' or, to quote one of my favorite reminders, *don't anticipate applause.*

Renunciation

Work toward loosening the bondage of attachment by discerning what causes harm and what is truly beneficial.

CHAPTER 2

MAGIC

The fox seems to grin as it gobbles up a hard boiled egg I've left outside my window. I often put a few scraps of food out there, as seeing an animal is one of the few opportunities for entertainment in the austere routine of this retreat. In the Fall I found a little mouse very engaging as he darted in and out of his home between the stones to get a bit of food. Now a deep snow covers everything and hopefully Mouse is cozy in his nest. Today, seeing this fox is rare, and it feels like a blessing.

I leave my room and go upstairs to the shrine room. It is a big space with a wooden floor on which are rows of meditation cushions and low tables to put our liturgies and chant sheets on. There are large shrines on each end as the room is sometimes divided into male and female sides. Thangkas of various deities and protectors hang on the walls. A few large windows offer a lovely view of the bay. There is always a faint smell of incense, even when none is actually burning.

Today Lama Tenzin is leading our group meditation session.
"Begin with the awareness of breath meditation," he says. Fortunately his English is quite good. "Sit upright, allow your mind and body to completely relax, but maintain clarity, or a relaxed vividness of mind."
We sit in silence for about 20 minutes, thoughts arising and departing in the spaciousness of complete presence. It is like an experience of small clouds passing by in a vast sky.

"Now you can begin investigating your mind and experience in very subtle detail. Yesterday we were looking for *who* exactly it is that is meditating, and today we are going to investigate whether it is the *mind* or the *body* that experiences sensations. This means *looking directly* at your experience, which is very different from merely thinking about this question."

I pinch my thigh and focus on the sensation. It feels like an experience of my body. But, if I pinch my leg while focusing on the birds flying over the bay the experience is quite different. Hmm.

We work with this question for the whole morning session, investigating various sensations. The process consists of settling the mind, looking at whatever the question of the day is over and over again, and then releasing all efforts and resting the mind.

After lunch, when the mail arrives, I'm surprised and delighted to receive a box of peanut butter cookies, sent from a friend back home. This is a rare event, since the postage to send something here usually costs more than the item being sent. Taking it down the hall I slip a note under Nora's door asking her to join me outside after lunch. Nora has become a dear and much needed friend here. She meets me out of sight of the building and we sit in the snow on the bubble wrap that had surrounded the cookies. In silence, we slowly eat this rare treat, smelling the strong peanut aroma, and savoring every crumb. Each time we lean over there is a loud POP.

As we gaze out over the bay I notice an occasional seal nose arising out of the water in the spaces where the ice has melted. Sometimes a whole seal becomes visible as it floats, belly up, for a few seconds. A few months ago we could peer through binoculars to observe the seals giving birth. The mother would come up onto the ice to have her pup, often surrounded by a variety of birds waiting for whatever bloody bits were left on the ice after mother and baby went back into the water.

Small, and I mean really small, miracles have been happening to me while I've been here. On several occasions, a thought about something I'd like to have crosses my mind, and then later that something shows up. When my birthday was approaching I thought 'wouldn't it be nice to have some blueberries.' Blueberries are highly unlikely to appear up here, at the end of the world, especially since no one knows I want them. Then Nora shows up, a package of frozen blueberries in hand saying "I was taken into town for emergency dental work and bought these for you."

An eerie amount of mind reading also happens in these kinds of retreats. Tom once told me that he dreamed about me - that I had met a man with long hair and a sizable nose and had become engaged. "Actually," I told him, "you are dreaming about my past. That already happened years ago, but we never got married."

Another time I thought 'I wish I had a long rope so I could get down the steep cliff and explore the shoreline in back of our retreat building.' This would mean *sneaking* down actually, since technically that would be out of the bounds of our retreat. Then a few days later *voila* - I found an old rope, apparently left there, under a bush near the cliff's edge, either by a retreatant from a previous year or by a workman. I tied it to the base of the bush and left it for later use, coiled up and covered with brush.

When I go outside, in the little time we are allowed, I become totally engrossed in each magical aspect of this stark and inhospitable place. I once followed a set of moose tracks in the snow into the woods and discovered a clearing with hoof prints circling around, branches broken off the lower parts of trees, small tufts of hair clinging to bushes, and droppings here and there. It looked like there had been a moose *hoedown* held by the light of the moon. Sometimes, when the wind is just right, I can smell a moose that is somewhere nearby. It is somewhat like oily, unwashed hair mixed with essence of rut.

These forays into the woods are not, strictly speaking, part of the retreat - it is assumed that the women are to stay in the small field next to our building. But, sometimes the combination of claustrophobia and love of the wilderness draws me into the forest. I'm always back by the time the next meditation session starts, and I try to disguise my tracks, so hopefully no one is noticing.

Another time I was startled to find a bird's beak lying on the snow. Perhaps an eagle had torn it from a raven and then eaten the rest of him. There is an intense primal quality in this wild, isolated place, where life and death are starkly displayed. When I get completely fed up with the relentless sameness of each day, I come to the cliff's edge, and sit on a milk crate, out of hearing range and hidden from the main house by bushes. Here I face the crashing surf and sing my heart out, sometimes random syllables, and sometimes the songs written by teachers of the lineage. Today's verse has been inspired by writings of Lord Gotsampa, about keeping an uplifted mind even though we are trapped on the endless wheel of suffering, called samsara. Fortunately the path of meditation and compassion offers a way to get off this wheel.

*When samsara is tormenting me,
Instead of staying in misery,
I focus on compassion
And delight in taking on the sufferings
Of other beings.*

Sachi Deleg

Magic

Clearly seeing what is actually there, rather than what the conceptualizing mind projects, is the essence of ordinary magic.

CHAPTER 3

HOOKED

BOOM, BOOM, Boom, boom, boom... I'm the drummer for the evening chant session, and am keeping a brisk pace on the three foot painted drum that hangs sideways from a wooden stand. We generally rotate the various roles - chant leader (who also wields the cymbals), drummer, and horn player. The chants in the evening involve making offerings of food, tea, water, and music to the protector deities. The protectors are depicted in Tibetan art as wrathful, with hair standing on end, eyes blazing, fangs bared (sometimes holding weapons), using whatever means necessary to subdue ego and support awakening. It is a form of "wrathful compassion," using the fierce qualities of kindness to overcome laziness, arrogance and other negative personal qualities. We supplicate these external representations of our own mind to assist us in our meditation. There is also a recognition that the external world is not dead space, and that there is a lively energetic quality to the unseen world that can be invited to help us.

The protector chants are generally recited at dusk, which is considered to be a time when the mind is particularly vulnerable. I notice Hector is writing a note that he passes over to Tracy. She reads it and smirks. It seems to me to be a particularly ludicrous time to be ignoring the chants - when we are in the midst of asking these somewhat fierce and wrathful beings to help us. I remind myself of one of the 47 ways a bodhisattva fails - by rejecting those who do not keep their discipline - and continue drumming. Boom, boom, BOOM!

After finally getting to bed, and gratefully falling asleep, I'm awakened by a vibration under my mattress. Groggy, I open my eyes into the pitch black of my room and try to make sense of what is happening. Then it dawns on me - someone is clomping around in the bathroom next door. Pushing the glow button on my watch reveals that it is 3:30 a.m.. I drag myself out of my down filled cocoon, and go over there. Jema is washing a lump of something that looks like socks in the sink and each time she presses down she lifts off the floor and slams her heels back down.

"What the hell are you doing?" I snarl, not awake enough to guard my tongue.

"I couldn't sleep," she retorts, "and I wanted to get this washing done - what business is it of yours?"

I draw in a breath. "I've told everyone at least three times that the wall separating the bathroom and my room is paper thin and making noise in here wakes me up. Could you do your washing during the day?" Jema just grumbles something under her breath and keeps going. I turn to leave and see that Nora and Tracy have been woken up by our interchange and are standing in their doorways to see what's up. "I'm going to strangle her one day," I mutter as I march back into my room.

Sleep is out of the question, so I put away my bed, light a candle and sit on my meditation cushion, trying to calm down. 'It wasn't supposed to be like this,' I think to myself, 'how did I get stuck in a group with such awful people?'

Breathe in, breathe out, breathe in, long breath out. Feel the earth, relax and let go. Expand into the space around you. Feel compassion, at least for yourself. Change your attitude and be with what is.

As the day progresses I still feel the repercussions of the interchange with Jema. We each have given up a lot to be here - left family and friends, jobs, homes and possessions. It is wonderful, but also very daunting to be so "free and well favored" as to be able to spend a year in retreat. Many people idealize this notion, imagining it to be so peaceful, while others think it is a ridiculous self indulgence or a waste of time. My view is that if you transform your consciousness in a positive way, even a little, it will be of benefit to yourself and others throughout time.

Speaking of family, I got a letter letting me know that my sister-in-law's mother died. By the time this news reaches me almost two weeks have passed, but I want to express my condolences. When we have a moment of free time I go find Lama Tenzin and ask him if I can call my sister-in-law Sophie. He agrees to lend me his cell phone for a "compassion call," but I have to go away from the building, out of sight and hearing range of the others.

I take the phone up to the trash shed to make the call. By some miracle I reach Sophie directly and we commiserate for a while. Beyond extending my sympathy there is not much to talk about. I'm standing in a dark, stinking, freezing cold trash shed, and have been spending twelve hours a day meditating, so not a lot of conversation nuggets embedded there. However it is great to connect to the outside world and maintain some family ties.

Sachi Deleg

Hooked

*Like a fish seeing a tasty morsel,
We get hooked by our own delusions
and negative emotions.
Examine but don't bite the hook.*

CHAPTER 4

FEAST

"Lama Tenzin, I feel like a bird circling and circling but not able to land." We are sitting in the shrine hall, facing each other for a meditation instruction session.
"You need to bring your awareness fully into your body," he says, and then he leans over and gently taps the center of my chest. A wave of deep sorrow wells up, and tears start streaming down my face.
"You can open to whatever feelings arise, without rejecting them or being captured by them," he continues, "feel them as a flow of energy."

The sorrow slowly subsides and I take a few deep breaths. It feels like an unconsciously held weight has lifted off of my chest. "Thank you," I say, "that was very helpful. I feel much more grounded, more embodied. It seems like there are endless layers of historical imprints that arise, and hopefully are released, when we open to the vast space of meditation."

"Yes," he replies, "our bodies are the storehouse of lifetimes worth of habitual tendencies that get illuminated by meditation. One aspect of the feast practice we will be doing today is to make an offering of all of our ego centered delusions, in addition to the physical offerings of flowers, incense, candles, food, and so on."

We bow to each other to end the session and I head down to the kitchen to help with preparing the meal. The feasts happen several times a month, scheduled according to the lunar calendar. The feast practices seem to be able to both energize and to pacify my state of mind, and it helps bond the meditation community. On these days the whole group gets together in the shrine room on the second floor of the building to chant a feast liturgy and make the appropriate offerings. These kinds of practices are one of the ways Tibetan buddhism distinguishes itself from other forms of buddhism.

Buddhism came to Tibet when the king decided he'd had enough of all the tribal fighting and invited the renowned Guru Padmasambhava, a teacher from India to come and introduce the teachings of the Buddha. This was many years after buddhism had already spread from India to

Southeast Asia and then to China, Japan and Korea. The style of buddhism imported to Tibet included meditation forms that mixed the Indian traditions of the time with some of the indigenous shamanistic traditions of Tibet. Therefore, Tibetan buddhism includes such practices as visualizations and mantra recitations, in addition to the basic breath awareness meditation common to all the Buddhist traditions.

"Rotate the wrist, open the palm, rotate the wrist, open the palm. Touch the index finder to the thumb as you raise the other three fingers straight up." I'm in the basement, whispering to myself as I practice the mudras, or hand gestures that accompany the variety of offering substances. As the feast leader this time, I am studying the meditation text, and choosing an inspirational reading for after we finish eating. The rest of the group will be preparing the food and the tormas, which are ritual cakes made out of roasted barley flour, butter, sugar and alcohol. The intricate rituals that are part of Tibetan Buddhism allows every aspect of our being to be engaged - body, speech and mind, and the offerings provide good training in generosity.

During the feast preparation and practice our usual silence is relaxed further and we can talk normally to each other and offer poems, readings or short performances after the three or so hours of chanting the liturgy and eating the meal. Then we will return to silence and solitary practice.

Nora now joins me to talk about doing a skit together for today's feast.
"Well, what do you have in mind?" she asks, as she sits down on one of the dusty chairs in the corner.
"Let's use what we can find in the storage closet down here," I reply, opening the door and entering the walk-in space. "Hmm, two kinds of dried spaghetti - wheat and spinach, and here is some twine. This gives me an idea! You have a nice wool hat don't you?"
"Yes," she says, "so?"
"Here it is," I say, pulling the spaghetti out of the box and tying it into two bundles. "Put these under your hat so they stick out like pigtails, and wear a nice shawl. You are going to be the wealthy lady who asks Milarepa questions, and I'm going to use the green spaghetti to represent Mila's hair as a ponytail under the back of my hat. While he was in wilderness retreats he survived by eating the nettles that grew wild near his cave for so long that his hair probably did

have a green tint to it. I will put on a white sheet to represent the cotton robe he wore. When I go back to my room I will re-write a version of one of his poems and we can sing it as a duet."

We are all assembled in the meditation hall, sitting on cushions in front of long, low *puja* tables that hold our texts, bells, hand drums and other ritual implements. The women, Nora, Jema, Tracy and I are on one side of the room and the men, Tharpa, Hector, Guenther and Tom are on the other, facing us. Today we are doing the Vajrayogini feast practice. This loosely translates as "the indestructible feminine energy that transforms desire or grasping into compassion."

I ring the gong to signal the beginning of the silent meditation at the start of the feast. After about fifteen minutes I look around the room. Our one actual monk member of the group, Tharpa, has already fallen asleep. His chin rests on his ample body and his shaved head twinkles in the candle light. While he is not the sharpest knife in the monastic cutlery drawer, he has a kind disposition and strong devotion, and he gets along with everyone. This is a very treasured quality here, and I appreciate him very much. Tracy, the youngest member of the group, is staring at Guenther. She has been flaunting herself in front of him rather obviously, even though we have taken vows of celibacy. My suspicion is that he has not been immune to these overtures.

I clear my throat to signal the beginning of the liturgy, and off we go. Almost immediately Jema starts competing with me by loudly trying to change the tempo of the chanting. She often does this to annoy whoever is leading, and ignores requests for her to harmonize with the rest of us. I pretend I don't notice and eventually she gives up.

Perhaps Jema's insecurities are understandable, given what I've heard her say about her difficult childhood. Her father abandoned the family when she was young, leaving America and returning to Europe. She never heard from him again. Even so, I'm sorry to say that I believe a few of the people that were accepted into the retreat got recommendations because their teachers were at their wits end about what else to do with them.

We move through the sections of the text - devotional passages, praises, offerings, visualizations, mantras, meditation, and requests for help in traversing the path. In the Tibetan cosmology, the world is considered very alive with various energies - almost entities, so to speak - that can be communicated with and can aid the meditation practitioner.

At the end of the chanting the meal is served. It is a little more interesting than our usual fare, and I am very grateful to have it, especially as it has been five hours since I have had anything to eat. We even get served chicken. Our usual fare is vegetarian, but we get meat on feast days. Tibetan Buddhists traditionally have eaten meat, largely because it is too cold in Tibet to get enough food otherwise. The stipulation is that the practitioner should be "two hands away" from the killing of the animal. This means you are not supposed to kill the animal, nor should it be killed specifically for you. There is some tricky logic here, but since I can't digest milk products I am grateful to have the additional protein, so I am a happy omnivore.

After a few minutes of savoring in silence I mention that it is okay to talk a bit. Hector brings up a question. "Why is OM so often at the beginning of our mantras?"

"I can answer," says Tom, waving his fork in the air. "OM is a *seed syllable*. Everything has to have an origin, and so from open space a sound vibration arises. In the case of OM, it actually has three aspects, *A, U*, and *M*. "*A*" represents arising, "*U*" abiding, and "*M*" dissolving. Everything that comes into our mind goes through that process, and if we recognize that, we are less likely to buy into what the conceptualizing mind comes up with, and can learn to see it like a bubble arising in the space of awareness and then disappearing, without any real substance."

"Nicely put, Tom," I say, and we go back to focusing on our food and individual conversations for a while. Tom has caught my attention as someone who is a genuinely decent and caring person. He also has a rather handsome face, but with me looking like a plucked chicken I've completely let go of the idea of attracting male attention. Besides, he is married. I have had a few relationships, but have never quite made it to getting married. Life as a single woman has had many advantages in terms of being able to do as I please, and has afforded me many opportunities to pick up and go into retreat, or to go live in a meditation center for a few years. However, I admit that loneliness has been a constant companion.

As we are finishing eating I remind people of the story of Milarepa in preparation for our song. "Milarepa was one of the most beloved meditation masters in Tibetan history. He had a rocky start in life when his father died and his family's wealth was stolen by an aunt and uncle, effectively making him, his sister and his mother into beggars. His mother encouraged him to learn black magic in order to get revenge. He was so adept at it that he brought down great weather related damage, causing the death of many people. He later felt such remorse that he begged one of the Buddhist masters to take him on as a student and to allow him to devote the rest of his life to the dharma to make amends. This teacher put him through great physical and mental trials, but Milarepa's determination led him to attain enlightenment in one lifetime. He gained fame from the 100,000 songs he wrote describing his long retreats in mountain caves, and his meditative realizations. Nora and I are going to sing a version of one of his songs."

We get up and go into the hallway to put on our costumes, then return and stand in front of the shrine. There are a few titters from the audience, as admittedly we look quite strange.

"In case it isn't obvious," I say, "I am playing Milarepa, and Nora is Lady Palderbum, a wealthy women who has meditation questions for Milarepa."

Nora starts with "*I can marvel at the sea, but waves unnerve me. Milarepa, will you tell me how to meditate on waves?*"

I chime in. *"If the sea is so marvelous, aren't the waves just the play of water? Let your mind rest within the sea."*

"I can appreciate the sky, but the clouds disturb me. Milarepa will you tell me how to meditate on clouds?"

"If the sky is so vast how could clouds be of concern? Let your mind rest within the sky."

"When it comes to my mind the many thoughts distract me. Milarepa will you tell me how to meditate on thoughts?"

"If you recognize your true mind, thoughts are just its display. Let your mind rest within itself."

As we are singing I notice Guenther is scowling, arms crossed over his chest. He thinks singing is foolish and refuses to participate when we sing as a group. The rest of us are enjoying ourselves and it makes for a lovely end to this day's feast.

Feast

*Rest your mental commentary and practice
directly seeing, hearing, tasting, smelling, and
touching.
Be fully present in each moment.
Then enjoy the world as a feast for the senses.*

CHAPTER 5

IMPERMANENCE

Today we are having a group work period to clean up the yard, pick up dead branches, and try to foster the few living bushes that have survived the deep snow that buries them every year. Tom wanders over to where I'm shaping a shrub and asks to talk to me. "Sure, what's up?"
"I got a letter from my wife," he says, staring intently at the ground. He pauses and sighs. "She has fallen in love with someone else and is leaving me. She is under the impression that telling me while I'm in retreat is a kindness since I can use all this meditation practice to heal." He looks up, tears in his eyes. "I knew going into retreat for a year was going to be hard on our marriage, but we discussed it, a lot, and she said she supported the idea. I can't believe this happened. It is already so hard to be here...I don't know what to do."

This is heartbreaking, and I automatically start to slow my breathing, feeling the sorrow and compassion this brings up. Tom is such an attractive, warm and intelligent guy, it is puzzling how someone could so easily let him go. I reach out and take his arm, steering him toward a quiet corner of the yard.

"Let's just sit down together in silence for a minute," I say, finding a dry spot for us to land on. We sit, cross legged, shoulder to shoulder, facing the bay. I silently invoke the nature "goddesses" to help - the stability of the earth to provide comfort for Tom, the flow of the water to ease his pain, and the expanse of the sky to free his mind from negativity. Tom is now openly weeping, which is a good sign.

"This is a place to go ahead and feel the hurt and the sadness, to take whatever time you need to be angry and to grieve," I whisper softly. "I'm so sorry this is happening to you, especially here where it is already so difficult and lonely. All of us will be here for you, even in our silence, and we are surrounded by countless higher beings that will hold you in compassion. Since we don't have many talking opportunities, maybe taking some time every day to write about whatever you are feeling will help." My psychotherapist side is starting to gear up, and I have to actively turn it off. A caring friendship is what will be the most beneficial here, and I'm happy to be able to extend a hand. "Also, I'm sure Lama Tenzin will talk to you whenever you want."

I notice Jema eyeing us, wondering what we are up to. I'll leave it up to Tom to tell the group or not in his own time. The outside gong is ringing so we have to finish up and go back inside for the next meditation session.

"Take heart Tom," I say, "bad relationships create great yogis." That gets a small smile, and we each walk to our side of the building. My heart goes out to Tom. What a horrid thing to have happen. I plan to do some healing visualizations for him, and hope he finds the strength to continue the retreat.

I decide to do Chöd meditation practice during this session in my room. It is a unique sadhana, or liturgy, that was created by Machig Labdron, one of the few females to be recognized as an exceptional teacher. The text consists of a series of visualizations designed to reduce attachment to our physical body, thus preparing us for the final separation experienced at the time of death. I find the text on the shelf, but the mala that is usually in the same cloth cover is missing. It is a unique mala I use only for this liturgy as it is made of small skull shaped beads carved out of animal bone. I search around, shaking the brocade text cover upside down, but nothing emerges. This is frustrating. I went to a lot of trouble re-stringing the beads with extra strong metal reinforced thread so it wouldn't break like so many of the other malas I've had, sending beads skittering across the floor in the middle of group practice sessions. 'Oh well, the practice is all about non-attachment so I may as well let it go and use my sandalwood mala.'

Impermanence

Objects appearing outside,
Inside, your mind flitting about,
And even your own body -
All are constantly changing.
Look deeply into what you can
Truly rely on.

CHAPTER 6

DESIRE

It is American Thanksgiving day, and we got permission to cook a turkey and make other traditional dishes. Being so far from home and from family, taking the time to celebrate familiar traditions is very comforting. Nora says she has cooked many turkeys for her family and so she is taking the lead in the meal planning. Hector has volunteered to make a Spanish custard that will hopefully compliment the pumpkin pie.

I'm heading to the basement storage closet to look for the cranberry sauce. Opening the door I'm startled to find Tom in there perusing the shelves. A crooked grin appears on his face as he turns to face me. Since we are still in silence I'm somewhat muddled about what to do. Tom very slowly leans over, gently places his forehead against mine, and closes his eyes. We just rest like that, feeling the melting quality of attraction pervade our bodies as we simply breathe together. Then he straightens up and slides past me and out of the door. A deep sigh escapes my lips as I pick up a large can of cranberry sauce and head to the kitchen.

There is a festive feeling as we all gather to dine together in the shrine room. We sit on meditation cushions on the floor, and put our plates on the long black puja tables. I've made some fresh flower arrangements for the shrine, and even though dark clouds are hovering outside, the candles are adding a warm glow. The smells of the wonderful combinations of foods are intoxicating.

I take a few breaths to relax and observe the beauty of the meal. The first bite is a brilliant burst of tastes and textures, the sharp cranberry against the mild white meat and touch of salty gravy. It brings pleasure and delight. I'm riding the razor's edge between appreciation and attachment and pay close attention, recalling, of the *Thirty-four Contradictions to Embodying Virtue,* the *contradiction to benefiting oneself,* which is mindlessly indulging.

Formerly, as a psychotherapist, I contemplated the nature of addictions quite a bit. This included the more hidden addictions to things like work, television or computers, as well as the more obvious addictions to substances such as alcohol, tobacco, and food. It all starts out so simply, as a bit of pleasure or relief, which the mind then starts clinging to in order to extend ordinary pleasure or to avoid or cover over pain. It then becomes a "devoted habit," or addiction. It is quite easy then to mistake excessive pleasure, and/or the avoidance of uncomfortable feelings, for happiness. What is interesting is that there are virtues that also stimulate the pleasure centers of the brain, including prayer, voluntary exercise, giving to charity, and, fortunately, meditation.

After a great meal like this it is a perfect time for a good joke. I turn to Nora who is seated on my right. "Would you like to hear a Buddhist knock, knock joke?" I ask innocently.
"Sure," she says.
I say, "You start."
Without thinking she immediately obliges me with "Knock, knock."
"Who's there?" I reply.
The stunned look on her face is priceless - pure satori. We both laugh and laugh.

After a delightful evening I make my way back to my room. As I change into the long cotton gown I sleep in, a strong memory arises of the week before coming to this retreat. I am shopping in a mall for last minute items to take into retreat when my attention becomes completely riveted. Hanging alone in a store's spotlight, is a pair of the most striking and lovely red silk pajamas I have ever seen. I'm drawn closer and closer until my hands reach out and touch the buttery soft fabric, thick and lush. It is a deep, throbbing red, and trimmed on cuff and hem with beautifully woven oriental brocade. My chest is tight with longing. 'Wake up!' an inner voice says. 'You are going into a monastic retreat for a *year*! You will be hairless, for god's sake, not to mention celibate. What on earth will you do with red silk pajamas?' True, all too true. But nonetheless I remain captivated. The tension of desire is palpable, my senses on high alert. Why am I doing this to myself?

Finally, my many years of meditation training begin to kick in. *Do not reject longing desires nor accept any attachment to desires.* I start to observe, without judgment. As the Buddha said, my eyes are on fire with wanting. My mind is lit up with associations and memories and has projected an elaborate storyline onto this cloth. I've been captured by a deeply engrained urge to engage in the play of attraction, the promises of sensuality, of pleasure, of love. And why not?

'Well, my dear, there is that small problem of impermanence, of change, and of the fact that you are aging faster than you would like to admit.' What do I truly want in this life? I have looked closely at the results of fueling the fires of sensual pleasure, and while admittedly dazzling, it is much like drinking ocean water - the more you drink the thirstier you get. If I can see this process clearly as it is, without the usual responses, there is the potential of breaking the chain reactions that keep me bound in suffering.

Meditation practice can bring a cooling breeze to the intense heat of craving, and it can allow a glimpse of the inherent peace at the core of our being. Then there is the possibility for the compelling energy of "wanting" to be motivating rather than burning - motivating toward wisdom and toward truly loving others.

Even beyond my own internal struggle, where exactly *is* the thing I want? Is it the color? Like a mirage in the desert, the red appears, but changes with each shift of the light. It is impossible to pin down what color is actually there. Further, what possible difference could "owning" red make - it freely exists everywhere.

What about the fabric? If the seams were to unravel and the pieces separate, they would hold no interest. Somehow, when joined together all the "pajama" associations arise and we follow attraction, rejection or indifference, like a cow pulled by a ring in its nose. On closer inspection, some of the seams are crooked, and others are already loosening. *All composite things will eventually fall apart, all that comes together will separate.* And this doesn't even take into account the inevitable food stains that will befall this illusion of perfection if it comes into my possession.

A more relaxed, discerning awareness begins to infiltrate my experience. Even though these pajamas are "empty" of the projections my mind has automatically applied, the appearance can still be appreciated, enjoyed as it is, and released. Even further, I can leave it for others to enjoy and rejoice in the pleasure it may bring them. My hands can now open rather than grip. My heart can feel full rather than needy, and my mind can relax.

I give a nod of appreciation to this sturdy blue nightgown I'm wearing and crawl gratefully beneath the covers. Of the Thirty Four Contradictions to Embodying Virtue I have made a small step toward *not remaining in the grip of samsara due to desire and attachment.*

Desire

Not getting what you want creates suffering.
Getting what you want may also be a form of suffering.
Look closely.

CHAPTER 7

APPEARANCE

It is 7:25 and I have been meditating since the morning gong tore me from my sleep. I've been waking up at five in the morning every day to start my meditation practice, done sitting in a meditation "box," which is part of the Tibetan Buddhist retreat tradition. What the box actually consists of is a wooden platform raised about a foot off the floor and big enough for a set of meditation cushions - a large flat one that supports my crossed legs (a zabuton) and a small round one on top of it that I sit on (a zafu). Also made of wood are a back panel rising about three feet above the platform and three sides that are about ten inches high, thus the term box.

We retreatants sit there for all of the meditation sessions that are done in our own rooms, and are also supposed to sleep sitting up, leaning on a pillow placed against the back of the box. The theory is that you will not fall as deeply into the animal-like ignorance associated with sleep if you are sitting up. I agree with that theory, but after three nights of sitting upright my crooked spine gave out and I could no longer walk. So, sleeping on a mat on the floor wedged between my box and the shrine has had to suffice for me, since we have no beds in our rooms. A cold breeze from the windows routinely flows along the floor, and my knees have not been pleased.

I take off my comfy blue nightgown and start layering up for the pre-breakfast exercise half hour outside. Woolen long underwear top and bottom, beige stretch pants, shirt, thick burgundy sweater, double layered socks, long down coat, scarf, thick gloves, boots, and a raggedy fur hat with ear flaps that my father brought back from a trip to Russia twenty years ago make up my ensemble. During the night a fine layer of snow has blown in and sits on the window latch, so my guess is that it is about twelve degrees fahrenheit out there. I'm committed to venturing outside every morning to do lujong no matter what the weather, and it has included opportunities to be blown over and to exercise in sleet carried horizontally into my face by fierce winds. *Lu* - body and *jong* - training is a vigorous form of Tibetan yoga performed standing up. My somewhat stern Tibetan teacher insists lujong should be done with bare feet, but I'm not going that far up here. Besides, I am not a hardy

Tibetan, but rather a middle aged American woman with a delicate constitution. Surviving this retreat is enough of a challenge for me.

The sky has cleared and the morning sun is reflecting brightly off of the snow. There is a deep silence but for the ice creaking on the bay. As I swing my arms side to side I notice a brilliant burst of deep blue on the ground a hundred feet or so from me. Sapphires on the snow? Could it be? Crunching through the icy crust I get close enough to see what it is, and have to laugh. Before me is a wet, sparkling wrapper from an S.O.S dishwashing pad, reflecting an intense blue in the sunlight. A flash of absolute truth occurs as the mind sees through its constructs. All that is really there is shape and color. In a way, this reflection from the wrapper is no different, in terms of direct perception for the awake mind than the appearance of a sapphire. It is only the conventional mind mired in relative reference points that makes up a world of difference.

I get back to huffing and puffing through the exercises and then sprint into the building to get oatmeal and take it to my room for a silent meal.

BAM! The bathroom door slams into my wall and I am treated to the sounds of Jema performing her morning gargling and spitting routine. Sigh. A good opportunity to practice separating sound and concept. After breakfast, the rest of the day will be about the same as most other days - meditate until lunch, eat, do my housekeeping job, meditate, have tea, meditate, eat dinner, meditate, and then fall onto my floor mat at 9:00 for the blissful sleep of an ignorant animal.

As my afternoon meditation winds down, the kitchen gong rings, signaling that the evening meal is ready. I finish the last set of mantra recitations and just sit for a moment. It dawns on me that it is the men's night to cook. We alternate, two women fixing dinner one night, two men the next. This puts somewhat of a damper on my enthusiasm for dinner. Rarely have they rallied to the occasion, but one can always hope. Making my way into the dining area, I pick up my bowl and utensils from the shelf. Everyone has a small shelf where they keep their own placemat, napkin, plate, bowl, utensils and cup. We wash and dry our own dishes and linens, and store them here. The

elegant Japanese red lacquer bowl I brought
cheers me up.

Scanning the serving bowls on the counter I
notice there is a large quantity of something
brown and lumpy. The cooks have fled back to
their side, so there is no one to explain what
we've been served. I look at Nora and she
shrugs, stifling a giggle. Everyone turns around
and heads back to their rooms for a can of
whatever is stashed for such an occasion. I check
my inventory. Hmm, let's see, tuna and crackers
seems just the ticket. I decide to eat by
candlelight, and fire up the glass oil lamps on my
shrine. Sitting in my box, I observe my meal,
placed neatly on the wheeled table that slides
over my lap. Separating a small portion of this
meager meal as an offering, I feel gratitude for
the fish that gave her life so that I have enough
nourishment to continue on my path. Then,
holding up my plate I chant:

> *"I pay homage to the Buddha*
> *I pay homage to the Dharma*
> *I pay homage to the Sangha.*
> *Please help clear obstacles*
> *on my path to full awakening.*

Tomorrow Nora and I will be the cooks. We are supposed to re-use any leftovers lingering in the refrigerator. However, desperate times require desperate measures so the brown goo just might accidentally slip into the compost bucket and find its way over the cliff and into the bay. Watch out any of you sea creatures with touchy digestive tracks!

Appearance

*Mirages made of hopes and fears
constantly dance before our eyes.
Settle your mind and see clearly
what **this** moment holds.*

CHAPTER 8

PURIFICATION

Today is our New Year celebration. It is supposed to be our one day of the year that we have "off," but in truth the whole day is packed with rituals and preparations for the celebration.

The morning is starting with a lhasang, which is a smoke offering. My job is to build the fire in the fire pit in back of the building. Firewood has been stored under a tarp for this purpose. I coat a few of the twigs with cooking oil and build a small pyramid over a bit of brush. Once this starts blazing bigger pieces are added until there is a fairly substantial bed of coals.

I give the signal that the fire is ready and everyone gathers outside. Standing in a circle around the fire, we are still quite cold, stamping our feet and pressing our hands into pockets. Jema volunteers to read a verse of devotional prayer:
"The wisdom mind inherent in all
is beyond meeting and parting.

Yet I still long for the presence of the guru."

It is heartfelt and reminds me that as annoying as Jema is, she also aspires to be liberated from suffering. I begin placing the juniper branches that have been gathered and soaked in water onto the fire. This immediately creates a billowing plume of fragrant smoke, which invites the dralas, or higher beings, to join us. Nora tosses offerings of tea and small specially made cakes into the fire for these invisible beings. The smoke also serves to purify the environment as well as ourselves. Anything we want to cleanse or bless can be passed through the smoke - texts, malas, religious statues, and so on.

This type of ceremony originated from the pre-Buddhist religion of Tibet, the Bön tradition, which has many shamanic elements and a deep connection to and respect for the natural world. We all walk in a circle around the fire, chanting and waving banners and flags. When we are done, Tom and I hang long strings of new multi-colored prayer flags between the trees, sending the blessings printed on them to ride the wind out into the world. He seems to have cheered up considerably since we last spoke, and I am enjoying this opportunity to have a few playful moments together.

"Tom, I'm so glad you have stayed in the retreat, even though I know it has been rough," I say. "I hope this new year brings a lot of happiness your way."

"You know," he replies, stopping to look directly at me, "you are one of the reasons I'm still here."

My eyes grow wide and a blush of red flies up to my cheeks. I feel a warm glow in my heart, and a deep appreciation for this man. I smile, and we go back to hanging the flags.

On this beautiful day, all of the elements come together as a gigantic offering - the fire and its smoke, the water in the bay, the earth, and the crisp, cold air. I notice Guenther is missing, which seems to enhance the opportunity for gaiety and lighthearted fun. I do wonder, though, what he is up to.

Purification

When we are able to look beyond ego
We can see the true sacredness and brilliance
Of the world.

CHAPTER 9

ILLUSION

The spray of a whale shoots up out of the bay. Seeing any of nature's wondrous displays is a welcome break in our austere routine. Today the women are having a group lunch on our side of the building, and I have been fortunate enough to get a seat that looks out over the water. We have come out of a long period of silence, but I am not looking forward to being able to speak. Although the first few days of stopping verbal exchange feels very lonely, I have grown to love the spacious peace that comes with a long silence, in this case three months. The living, awake quality of the world is able to seep in and enliven me in ways that disappear when I'm immersed in language.

Jema hasn't shown up for lunch, which is highly uncharacteristic of her, and in fact is an event with no precedent in the 10 months we have been cloistered here. I volunteer to go check on her, assuming she is asleep, which *would* be very characteristic, sorry to say, in this case. As is my habit, I mentally apply an antidote to my ill will toward Jema. *May she be well, may all good things come to her, may my heart be open and kind to all beings.*

There is an ancient story about a Buddhist teacher who was invited to bring the dharma teachings to Tibet. He had heard that the Tibetans were extraordinarily good natured people, and he was concerned he would have no opportunities to practice *tonglen* - taking in the suffering and disturbing qualities of others and offering out relief from suffering and compassion in exchange. To make sure he had enough irritants along to aid his determination to practice kindness, he deliberately invited a very bad tempered and annoying young man who was the tea preparer to go with him, much to the chagrin of others in the traveling group. It turned out however, as with all human societies, that there were plenty of irritating Tibetans.

Jema is our resident "tea boy." She goes out of her way to disturb our periods of silence, she is belligerent if she doesn't get her way, and she is often heard wandering the halls when we are supposed to be in our rooms meditating. She has wooden soled shoes and has refused all requests not to wear them during the retreat, so we can hear her heavy treads night and day. As a trained psychotherapist, I unfortunately can recognize a neurotic quality from a hundred paces, and am trying hard not to label her as one of the personality disorder diagnostic categories. *May she be well.*

As I reach her room, I tap lightly on the door, to no response. One of the many rules of retreat is that we are not supposed to go into anyone else's room, another way Jema routinely violates our structure. I open the door just enough to peer in. One naked leg is hanging at a crooked angle over her meditation box. As I come in to the tiny room I see her maroon robes in disarray and her head hanging unnaturally close to her chest, blue and red blotches coloring her exposed neck. My mind completely stops. When it comes back online the first thought is 'She looks dead.' One more item rivets my attention. I blink a few times just to make sure that what I think is appearing is really there. Around her neck is a mala that has apparently been used to strangle her. Not just any mala, but one with skull beads, just like the one that disappeared from my room.

"*Om mani padme hum*" springs to my lips, the well practiced mantra in response to any startling event. I reach over to feel her arm for any pulse.

Her pale wrist is cold to the touch. She had been the "lucky" one who got the corner room - three windows instead of two - but the effect was that the room stayed chilly all winter long. In Nova Scotia, that meant ten months of the year. Apparently she had been dead long enough to have lost all internal heat. Even though Jema had been a really troublesome and annoying part of our retreat, deep sorrow wells up as I see her like this. *Om mani padme hum* - the jewel is in the lotus. *Jema, even in death may you realize your Buddha nature, rising out of, and unstained by, the muck of this confused and troubled world.* Tears start to run down my cheeks as I take a few deep breaths.

With a sigh I walk back to the dining room, let the others know, and ask Nora to call the police and Tracy to go find the retreat master. Heading back to Jema's room I review in my mind the Tibetan Buddhist practice of *phowa*. This is a way of reminding the dead person's consciousness to rise and leave the body through the top of the head in order to connect with the mind stream of the enlightened ones. It makes it more likely the consciousness can then move on to a higher realm, or at the very least take a consciously chosen rebirth again on this earth. This is helpful to do as soon after death as possible, although it is believed the dead person's consciousness may take as many as 49 days to find it's next home. Many of the advanced tantric Buddhist meditations include visualizations of the subtle network of inner channels and methods for clearing any blockages so that consciousness can move freely into the central channel. At the time of death it then leaves the body via this channel, through the top of the head.

Standing close to Jema's head, I recite a verse about death out loud, hoping it may encourage her to use what she has learned to navigate her journey:

"When it's time to depart the illusionary tangle - this body,
Don't wallow in grief and anxiety.
What you should contemplate
Is that there is no true dying,
But rather the 'mother' clear light
Uniting with the 'child' clear light."

Waiting for the authorities I'm wondering how this could have happened. What possible motive could someone have for killing Jema, and how could they have gotten in, unnoticed, to our isolated building? We are bounded in the back by steep cliffs dropping down to a freezing cold bay, and in the front by a tall wooden fence and a road leading to the main monastery. The eight people in the retreat were all supposed to be sincere Buddhist practitioners who had been meditating for many years, and who had taken a bodhisattva vow, promising to help others towards enlightenment. While we may have occasional fantasies about killing each other, trapped together as we are in a very small space for a very long time, it is hard to imagine someone actually harming another person in such a vicious way.

In order to be eligible to even enter the retreat, all of us are supposed to have accomplished what are termed the four preparatory practices, or *ngöndro* as it is called in Tibetan. This consists of physically performing a prostration - going from standing to sliding oneself on one's palms along the floor until completely face down, arms stretched over head in a gesture of surrendering your ego - 100,000 times. This alone could take months to years of effort. Then comes reciting a one hundred syllable purification mantra 100,000 times, making a mental offering of all things valuable 100,000 times (mandala practice), and saying a mantra honoring the highest embodiment of wisdom 100,000 times (guru yoga). These practices were meant to pacify our mind enough to be able to take on the more advanced meditation practices that we were to do in this retreat.

Given this basis, it is very hard to imagine how one of us, who had dedicated much of our lives to cultivating a loving attitude toward others, could kill someone in cold blood. Also, I'm really disturbed that my mala was used to strangle her. How did it get out of my room, and who would want to so deliberately implicate me in this?

My pondering is interrupted by the police detective bursting into the room. He sees Jema slumped in her box. There are no chairs in the room, and I am sitting on the floor in what little space there is next to the window, so the detective has to stand against the wall. He is tall and solidly built, with clear blue eyes, a pleasing face, and dark hair left a bit longer than one would expect of a policeman. He takes a long look at Jema and the surroundings before finally speaking. "I'm Detective Connolly. Are you the one who found her, and is this the way she was found?" he asks.

"Yes," I answer, getting up to reach over Jema's outstretched leg and shake his hand. "I'm Rachel, one of the retreatants here. This is such a horrible thing to happen - we are all completely stunned." Tears are forming in my eyes and my voice catches in my throat as I try to get out the next sentence. "I need to tell you - the mala beads around her neck - they were mine. But I don't know how it got in here. It disappeared out of my room a while ago."

"What is it used for?" he asks.

"We do meditation practices that have mantras as part of them," I reply, "and when you have recited a certain number of mantras it is a marker that you can go on to a different practice if you wish. The malas are for keeping track of the number of mantras recited."

"Are there different kinds of these things or does everyone have the same type?"

"There are many different types of materials used for malas - wood, gemstones, crystal, and different sized beads, however this one is not very common."

Detective Connolly takes some photos, and examines what little there is in the room. Lama Tenzin pokes his head through the door. He looks ashen, apparently having been filled in on what has happened. When Detective Connolly asks the coroner to take the body away, Lama Tenzin volunteers to accompany Jema and perform the appropriate practices as best he can before she is autopsied. Usually we would try to keep the body for three days to say the appropriate prayers and give the person's consciousness time to depart, but in these circumstances they need to have the body for autopsy right away. "Alright," Connolly says, "but no one else is to leave the retreat site, and no one is to come into this room. This whole place is a crime scene. Someone from our team will be with Mr. Tenzin the whole time, and will bring him back here."

I guess we are all suspects. As I'm walking out, I glance at Jema's now empty meditation seat. It is a stark reminder of the uncertainty of this life, the truth of impermanence.

Back in my room I find I can't concentrate. The wind outside has picked up and is so strong it feels like the roof could be lifted right off, which only adds to my uneasiness. Part of a liturgy comes to mind that seems quite apt.

Death comes without warning, and this body will be a corpse. Then the dharma will be my only hope. I must practice diligently.

I decide to read the Tara liturgy, as she is a compassionate deity committed to helping all beings. She made a point of staying in female form from incarnation to incarnation to emphasize that women could also attain enlightenment. Calling on her, imagining her presence, and feeling her compassion usually has a calming and uplifting effect. Any merit gained from doing this practice I dedicate to Jema, *may her journey be one of peace.*

Illusion

This body will be a corpse.
This thinking mind is constantly changing.
Who then are we?

CHAPTER 10

INQUIRY

Detective Connolly has gathered all of us into the shrine room, the only place big enough for the seven people left to come together. We look quite glum, some of us still tearful. "This is truly a sad day, and I am sorry for the loss of your retreat companion," he says. "At this point we have very little to go on regarding who could have done this. Did any of you notice anything unusual today, anything at all?"

Nora, who has the room directly across the hall from Jema, speaks up. "When I went to throw my water offerings out of the side door I noticed the snow by Jema's window looked like it had been smoothed out. I first wondered if Jema had sneaked out of her room through the window, but truthfully I don't think she would bother to cover her tracks if she did. Maybe that is how the killer got in." Hmm.

I am observing the others as Detective Connolly talks. Tracy is crying. She was one of the few people here who got along with Jema. Hector is looking out of the window, either bored with the whole thing or trying to keep a neutral expression on his face. Guenther is staring at the floor and saying nothing. Tharpa turns his mala in his hand, bead by bead, saying mantras under his breath. I'm still wondering how my mala got into Jema's room and not liking the implications one bit.

Tracy pipes up. "A few months ago Rachel got really angry at Jema and said she would strangle her one day." Everyone turned to look at me.
"Is that true?" asked Detective Connolly, eyeing me a bit strangely.
"Well, I didn't actually mean I would do it - it was a figure of speech that I blurted out without thinking."

Nora speaks again. "What are you going to do to protect the rest of us? This building has no locks on any of the doors or windows. What if some lunatic is out there who wants to get rid of all of us?" The detective considers this and then tells us that he or a member of his police force will be walking the grounds at regular intervals. Having gotten very little useful information, he warns us about not leaving the retreat grounds.

As we are leaving the room Tom comes over and takes my hand. "I know you had nothing to do with this," he says, "Even though I imagine you are struggling with all that goes on here, you have a beautiful spirit and it always shines through." I'm very touched, and the warmth of his hand makes me feel comforted.

Back in my room I find I can't settle down, so I get out a pad and make a list of the retreat participants. Tom, a middle aged man from Wyoming, sometimes loses his temper but is then remorseful and apologetic. And, I'm growing very fond of him so I would very much appreciate it if he was not a murderer. Tharpa, the monk, rarely gets visibly aggravated, and shies away from conflict. Hector, our one representative from Spain, is fairly self-absorbed but causes little trouble for others. Then there is Guenther. I am suspicious of him. He seems to know very little about the Buddhist teachings and never offers any personal details about his life during our group feasts. Tom told me, in confidence, that he has seen Guenther playing computer games in his room - even though we are not supposed to even have computers.

On the women's side, there is Nora, who has been a great friend and confidant for me here, and I can't imagine she has the kind of aggression needed in order to kill someone. Tracy is young and immature, and she has a sharp tongue. When we are in the kitchen together, Nora and I sometimes take turns, one of us imitating Tracy while the other one practices staying calm and not reacting to the exceptionally annoying comments she routinely makes. However, she is the one who seems to like Jema the most.

Then, of course, there is me, but I know from experience that I'm no good at killing. Years ago I was meditating in a retreat cabin in the woods for a few months, and it was overrun with mice. When they started leaping onto my bed while I slept I had had enough, and put out a mouse trap. I actually caught one, but seeing it lying there with a broken neck resulted in a cascade of tears, on and off for the rest of the day. From then on I meditated inside during the day and slept outside at night. The meditation center eventually got rid of the mice, but in general, creatures are an integral part of living in remote mountain areas.

Another time I was woken out of a deep sleep by a loud grinding sound. Rousing my courage and getting a firm grip on my flashlight, I peered outside. A rotund porcupine, quills splayed in all directions, was happily munching on the cabin wall. Apparently the glue in plywood is a porcupine delicacy. "Get out of here!" I yelled - to absolutely no effect. Throwing firewood resulted in me getting a fierce glare while the animal slowly sauntered away - coming right back as soon as I was no longer visible. Eventually I figured out that dousing the cabin walls with mustard and pepper mixed with water took the pleasure out of gnawing the cabin and sleep was again possible.

What are the usual motives for murder? Passion is one. Jema was fifty-some years old, had a fairly off-putting personality, and had been here wrapped in maroon wool from head to toe for the past ten months. Plus, she had a shaved head, so I'm crossing "crime of passion" off the list. As far as I know, she had been divorced for many years and had no one waiting for her on the "outside." Revenge was a possibility, but why wouldn't the killer wait until she was back out in the world? Money is always a good bet. As far as I knew though, Jema had a comfortable income from a small business she owned, but nothing that merited this big of a risk. I'll have to sleep on it, and hope my mind can come up with something useful during the night.

Inquiry

Motivation lies at the root of our actions.
Examine carefully.
Be honest.

CHAPTER 11

ATTACHMENT

I'm floating in space, about five feet above my bed, when the gong rings and I wake up, on the floor as usual. Meditating so intensely for so long it sometimes feels like I could levitate right off my cushion. Such a strong connection has developed with the space and environment around me that I feel much less "this" oriented and much more accessible to "that," the very alive and vibrant space around me. It feels like I have plugged in to a different energy source and my perceptions are heightened and very sensitive.

After the 5 a.m. meditation session I dress and go outside for lujong. In the field next to the women's side of the building is a dead raven lying on the snow. Seeing such a beautiful creature lying so still and frozen hurts my heart. I have learned to distinguish ravens from crows by observing the "V" shape formed by the raven's tail as they soar in the air. Using some tissues from my pocket I pick it up and move it into the trees, placing it on a rock. *May your next rebirth be satisfactory.* The ravens seem to be protectors of our retreat, and for all I know they are already higher beings keeping an eye on us. They are smart, and often can be seen playing tricks or generally tormenting other creatures. A few minutes later about a dozen ravens gather in a circle, perched in the trees around the dead bird, and caw loudly for about ten minutes. Funeral accomplished, they then fly off in their separate ways.

Today we will be performing a Sukhavati ceremony in the shrine room in honor of Jema's death. A bottle of soda, her favorite drink, and a few cookies she was particularly fond of are placed on the shrine next to the other offerings. Tracy has provided a picture of Jema that has been attached to a small stick and placed upright in a bowl filled with sand. Tom is leading the ceremony, and starts with a few remarks about what he appreciated about her. "Jema had a strong commitment to the dharma, evidenced by her taking a year out of her life to come here. She had a quirky sense of humor, and could tell a good joke. I'm sure her friends and family will miss her."

I have volunteered to read a few passages from the Book of the Dead, which describes the dying process as well as the journey through the "in between," or bardo, states traversed by consciousness before it takes its next rebirth.

Now when the bardo before death dawns upon me,
I will let go of all grasping and attachment,
become undistracted regarding the teachings,
and eject my consciousness into the space of clarity;
as I leave this body of flesh and blood
I will recognize it to be transitory and an illusion.

Lama Tenzin speaks up. "Remember that the person going through the bardo is very sensitive and can perceive the thoughts of others and can also travel easily from place to place. It is very helpful to keep a serene, loving mind state to help Jema overcome the trauma of her death."

Tom then directs us to do twenty minutes of *tonglen* practice. Tonglen means "sending and taking." This is one of the practices of an aspiring bodhisattva, those of us who have taken a vow committing ourselves to helping all sentient beings attain enlightenment. Eyes closed, in silence, we imagine taking in the suffering and bewilderment of others, and then offering sanity and relief from suffering in return. I imagine taking in all of the difficulties that transpired between Jema and I, and offer her freedom from any disturbances or blame. After a few minutes I open my eyes and look around the room at the others. Most people appear sincere in their practice. This tragedy has been a great shock to us and we are each taking it to heart in our own way. Guenther however, is drumming his fingers on his leg, as if he can't wait to get out of here.

Living in such close proximity to others for this amount of time, we have become one organism. I can sense subtle changes in everyone else, as I'm sure they can "read" me also. My intuition tells me there is definitely something off about Guenther. I go back to my tonglen practice and include Guenther along with Jema. We recite a few more chants and then Tom strikes a match, sets fire to the photo of Jema and allows it to burn, symbolically freeing her from this realm.

While the others continue their meditation in the shrine room, Nora and I go downstairs to the kitchen and see what ingredients are available. Rice, vegetables, and tofu - oh, what a surprise. After measuring out the rice and putting it on the stove I tell Nora I'm going to clean off the table on the men's side. As soon as I get out of sight I slip down the hall to Guenther's room. The other men have left their doors open, but his is shut. This makes it harder for me to get up the nerve to enter, but my suspicions push me on. I turn the knob and, holding my breath, go in.

One of his windows is wide open, even though it is 30 degrees outside and the heat is on. This seems to be a European proclivity, as when I'm in the yard I've noticed Hector's window is also often open. On the floor are a number of mismatched socks, and a novel sits on his meditation cushion, with what looks like a title in another language. Dust covers the surface of the shrine and the fruit offering has gone moldy. I pick up the cloth covering the shrine and look underneath. A jumble of partially burned candles, some matches, and a few plates with food still crusted on them all crowd together.

I let the cloth drop back down and turn to the shelves next to his meditation box. A few cans of food - salmon and sardines, sit next to two boxes of wheat crackers. There is a large white notebook we all got when we arrived, that goes into great detail about the history and meaning of the variety of meditation practices we are doing.

This copy looks untouched. One shelf has some rumpled clothing stuffed into it, and the bottom shelf has a pair of black rubber boots and a pair of sneakers. The tiny "closet" - an open space with a few hangers - also holds little of interest.

This is getting me nowhere and my anxiety level is rising by the second. How many hiding places could there be in one little room? Maybe he is just an unsophisticated meditator with no manners and all my suspicions are just my own projections. Then my attention is drawn to the meditation box. Reaching over, I lift the cushions off and pull up the wooden seat. Jackpot! Sitting on top of a number of papers and books is a red passport. As I start to open it I hear footsteps coming down the hall. Quickly I shove the passport into my pocket, toss the cushions back on to the seat, and climb out of the window. As quietly as possible I crawl along the wall until I get to the front porch. After brushing the snow off of my pants I go in the front door and walk back into the kitchen.

Nora doesn't seem to notice that I went out in one direction and came back in through the opposite door. I start putting the food out on the women's side and Nora takes the rest of the serving bowls over to the men's side. I put a few food items into my bowl - rice, a mix of vegetables and some soy sauce. I'm too nervous to really pay much attention to what it is, and I head off to my room to eat in silence.

Attachment

Where does "mine" start and end? Attachment is the outcome of habitually ignoring what is, and the resultant suffering is worthy of compassion.

CHAPTER 12

CLARITY

After dinner, in my room I finally have the privacy to look at Guenther's passport. There is a photo of Guenther's face, but lo and behold, the last name is not the one he has told us. In fact, his last name is Berger, the same as Jema's. What could that mean? This may be the key to solving this murder, and I want to do everything possible to make sure whoever did it is caught, and also not be falsely accused myself. An idea starts to form. I set my alarm for midnight and put it under my pillow so as not to awaken anyone else. I don't bother changing into my night gown and just lie down fully clothed for a few hours of sleep.

Bzzzzz. I turn off the alarm and drag myself out of bed. Slipping on my black raincoat and boots I climb quietly out of my window. There is no moon, but the terrain is familiar. I creep as quietly as possible over to the gate, slide open the latch, and leave our compound. It feels pretty weird to be on the "outside." Moving quickly along the dirt road I make it to the monastery in just a few minutes. The nice thing about being so isolated is that nobody locks any doors. Everything is dark and silent as I sneak in to the main doors, make my way into the administrator's office and close the door. Her computer is still on, glowing on the desk. 'Come on, connect me to the internet.' When it comes up I put Guenther's real name and hometown in Switzerland into Google and push search. Connecting, connecting, and finally, connected.

What comes up is an announcement for a funeral in a local paper. It must be for his father. *Heinz Berger is survived by his wife Anne Marie and step-son Guenther Berger.* What could this have to do with Jema's murder? I'm going to contact Detective Connolly first thing in the morning and let him figure it out. I close down all traces of my search and slip out of the monastery. As I walk along the road my senses are on high alert. Every rustling sound coming from the bushes make my shoulders head toward my ears. I finally reach my window and crawl happily back into my room. This time I get into my night gown and snuggle into my "bed" and go to sleep.

"*Hchhhhh.*" Something is pressing on my neck and I wake up with a start. Guenther's angry face is about three inches from mine and his forearm is crushing my throat. "Where is my passport?! Do you think I don't know what you are up to?" I manage to signal that I will get it for him and he lets up on my neck. "Don't make a sound or I'll strangle you too."

Coughing and sputtering I get up and go over to the shelves near my door. He is holding on to the back of my night gown. It is obvious to me he'll probably kill me as soon a he gets the passport. When it is in my grasp I turn suddenly and elbow Guenther in the nose. All my lujong practice has made my arms strong and fast and I have taken him by surprise. It gives me enough time to open the door and dash out, heading for the side exit from the building.

Hitting the ground running I tear around the corner of the building, screaming for help. I can hear him behind me. "Shut up or you will be sorry!" he yells. It is really dark, but I can still see the outline of the cliff against the slight glow of the bay. Reaching the edge, I dive under the bush where my rope is tied, grabbing it and slipping down over the ledge. There had not been enough time to unwind the rope from the bush trunk, so I only have enough length to dangle over the cliff edge. If I let go it is going to be a fall of about 50 feet and a landing on sharp rocks.

Guenther can no longer see me and is stumbling around in the bushes, calling my name in a hoarse whisper. I am starting to freeze out here, not having put on a coat, shoes, or gloves, and my hands are cramping.

There is an old Zen tale about just this sort of situation. A man is hanging by a rope on a cliff. Below is a hungry lion, and above a mouse is starting to chew his rope. He sees a wild strawberry within reach, plucks it from its stem, and completely enjoys eating it, savoring its taste and the preciousness of that moment. I must admit, my mind is very alert and "in the moment," but I can't say I'm enjoying this. I whisper to the goddess Tara, who is committed to helping all beings. "*Om Tare Tu Tare Ture Soha.* Please give me the strength to hang on. Please help me." I try to find even a tiny foothold to get some relief for my frozen fingers but my toes cannot find any perch.

Finally, when all seems lost, I hear a big thump and the familiar and most welcome voice of

Detective Connolly. "Stop struggling so I can get these handcuffs on!"
Apparently he has subdued Guenther, who is angrily shouting for him to let go.

I take the opportunity to chime into the chaos with "I'm down here, help me!" Connolly got Guenther secured to a tree and located me. Lying flat on the ground he reaches over the cliff, grabs my wrists and hauls me topside. He takes off his jacket and wraps me up, while guiding me, shivering and stumbling, back into the building. "Send Mitch and Donaldson here. I think we have caught the killer," he says into his cellphone.

As we enter the kitchen, Nora's mouth drops open a she sees my filthy face and bloody hands. She has been awakened by all the noise and came into the kitchen to see what was happening. She hands me a damp towel and fixes us some tea while I tell the detective about my suspicions and the perhaps ill conceived sleuthing into Guenther's room. I still have the passport in my night gown pocket and hand it over. "You will notice he has the same last name as Jema," I say.

"Well," Connolly says, "with this I should be able to track down what the connection is to Jema's murder. I'm going to take him with me to the station, and there will be two policemen guarding this place for the rest of the night." Nora volunteers to bring some hot food to me in my room, and to let the others know what has happened.

I wash up, make my way to my meditation cushion and wearily flop down to try to make sense of this whole thing. Someone taps on my door. "I'm going to break the rules and bring in your food," Nora whispers. The smell and taste of warm soup is most soothing. "What on earth happened?" she asks.
"I've been suspicious of Guenther for a long time, so I went down to his room to snoop around," I answer. "Unfortunately he figured out that I had taken his passport and might have killed me too if I hadn't been able to get away from him."

"I'm so glad you are safe" Nora says, "but I sure wish you had told me what you were up to so I could have watched your back."
"Well, I was afraid you would think I was crazy, not to mention that I violated all the rules going in there. Being under suspicion myself has made me really want to get some answers about Jema's death. Apparently Guenther must have some

connection to Jema's father, and would somehow either benefit or exact some kind of revenge through killing Jema."

Nora nods thoughtfully. "It will be such a relief to finally clear all this horrible mess up. Here," she says, leaning over, "I brought some antiseptic cream and bandages. Let me help you get fixed up." When she leaves I manage to put my bed down, even with all my fingers bound together. I still feel shaken up, and put a box of shrine supplies against the door before lying down. Guenther has scared the hell out of me, and probably would have killed me too if he had caught me. Bodhicitta, or the heart of compassion, is hard to recall at a time like this, but I do feel sorrow that his "happiness" depended on doing such a heinous act. I recite a verse to help me gain perspective:

All being have been my mother and father. Recognizing this I train in love and compassion, let go of worrying about myself so much, and give rise to the heart of awakening, bodhicitta.

I renew a strong determination not to give in to hatred and not to allow my actions to be driven by fear. As I try to fall asleep, images of all that has happened keep flashing through my mind. I meet each one with compassion until I drift into a restless sleep.

Clarity

*Reasoning, intuition and insight
Arise from study, contemplation and meditation.
Logic alone will lead you astray.*

CHAPTER 13

RENEWAL

It is finally Spring! The temperature has risen to 35 degrees Fahrenheit, the sun is shining and this merits a celebration. I'm foraging through the basement freezer trying to locate the hot dogs and buns stashed there for such an occasion. 'Ah ha', found them. They will thaw in my room while I make the cookout preparations. A large empty can from the kitchen with holes punched into the sides - check. Small branches and weeds that have been hidden under the porch to keep dry - check. Matches and bits of paper - check. Two sticks and a knife to sharpen the ends - check. A few plastic bags for sitting in the snow finishes the supply list.

Nora and I take our booty out to the snow covered field to attempt our cookout. A merry fire gets going in the can (a little vegetable oil on the small pieces of wood works quite well to keep them burning). We each stab a sharpened stick into a hot dog and hold it over the flame. This is living - sitting on the sparkling snow savoring a blackened hot dog, gazing over the bay. The ice has broken apart and large chunks float by. An ice hockey net is still caught in one of the larger hunks and drifts along like some sort of ghost's playing field. Creatures of all kinds are starting to awaken from their deep winter slumber and birds are flocking back from the south. Besides the presence of the usual ravens, a red-tailed hawk circles slowly overhead.

"What do you think of what Detective Connolly told us last night?" Nora asks.
"Quite amazing," I reply. "Guenther managed to find out so much about Jema without her even suspecting he was the step son of her father. It is sad that both of them had such a miserable relationship with their father. Apparently he had enough remorse about leaving Jema's mother that he left Jema the bulk of his estate. Guenther found out about the will and was determined to get his share. It probably was no picnic being raised by this man. The only way he stood to inherit was if he got rid of her somehow. I bet he was hoping to find some way to make it look like an accident, perhaps shove her over the cliff. But when the elder Berger died recently the pressure

was on to move quickly." I stop to take another bite of food.

"He must have been keeping an eye out for the funeral notice, or perhaps he has been emailing some confidante all this time with his hidden computer," Nora comments.
I chime in - "Apparently he figured he could make it look like I did it, and then go back to Switzerland under his real name with no one the wiser. Wouldn't that be a horrid possibility - going to jail for a crime I didn't commit?" I shudder contemplating such a painful outcome.

It is quite the soap opera they have all been living, with broken marriages, an absent father, a large fortune at stake, and late life remorse. Who knows where the money will end up. I truly hope that Jema migrates toward an incarnation where she can continue to study the dharma, and that Guenther contemplates the outcomes of his greed and aggression and develops compassion, or at the very least remorse.

Renunciation is the foot of meditation. Do not be attached to food or wealth and sever the ties to this life.

Going to all of this effort for a hot dog does not exactly make us the poster children for renunciation, but a deeply held aspiration will hopefully keep us on the path.

And, then there is Tom. It remains to be seen how we will feel about each other when we return to the world. Having a companion on the path of dharma could be a beautiful experience. I hold no illusions (well, probably a few) about love, but I would be interested in bringing the richness as well as the provoking qualities of being a couple into my life. The idea of putting aside my own ego demands for the sake of another person would be a challenge, but one worth taking on.

I will miss Nora, who has been such a good friend and support. She has grown children, and wants to live near them. I think she will be a wonderful influence on her grandchild. If Tom and I continue to grow close to each other, perhaps we will go on a pilgrimage together, following the Buddha's footsteps in India and Nepal. Anything is possible, and after all the trauma we have all been through I feel thrilled just to be alive.

May all beings be well,
May all beings be content,
May all beings hold their sufferings in compassion,

Sachi Deleg

May all beings be at peace.

Renewal

*Relying on the Four Immeasurables,
Joy, Love, Equanimity, and Compassion,
That always exist within the heart,
Is the best way to proceed.*

ABOUT THE AUTHOR

The name Sachi Deleg is a pen name chosen for this book. The author has spent much of her life studying the teachings of Buddhism and practicing meditation. She has participated in many group and solitary retreats, and has been a meditation instructor at a number of retreat centers. The author has led many meditation programs in both the Tibetan Buddhist and Vipassana traditions. She is also trained as a psychotherapist.

To contact the author email
sachideleg@gmail.com
Please note that ongoing retreats may prevent a timely answer.